Yuletide Invasion

A Holiday Horror Novella

J.C. Moore

MissingStarBooks

Copyright ©2022 by J.C. Moore

All rights reserved.

No portion of this book may be reproduced in any form without written permission from the publisher or author, except as permitted by U.S. copyright law.

This is a work of fiction. Names, characters, places, and incidents either are the product of the author's imagination or are used fictitiously. Any resemblance to actual persons, living or dead, events, or locales is entirely coincidental Illustrations

Copyright © 2022 by J.C. Moore

Author photograph Copyright © 2022 by Heather Miller

Cover design Jorge Iracheta

ISBN: 979-8-218-09612-0

MissingStarBooks

Contents

Epigraph — V

Introduction — VII

1. Prologue — 1
2. The Blizzard — 6
3. The Accident — 19
4. The Newcomers — 27
5. The Shed — 32
6. The Intruder — 37
7. What Used To Be Geno — 44
8. Looking For Help — 50

9. The Showdown	54
10. Epilogue	60
Afterword	65
Acknowledgments	67
If you enjoyed the story	69
About Author	70
Also By	71

Still through the cloven skies they come

With peaceful wings unfurled,

And still their heavenly music floats

O'er all the weary world

It Came Upon The Midnight Clear

Introduction

One Christmas Eve in Upstate New York, an unlikely group of everyday people saved the world from unthinkable horrors. This is the story of their heroic triumph.

So, grab your favorite winter beverage, pull up a chair, and enjoy this holiday tale of a night when blood and snowflakes fell like confetti.

One

Prologue

"Tell me a Christmas story with the monsters, Grandma."

The woman in the rocking chair paused momentarily and looked into the fire. "It isn't a pleasant story, dear."

"Oh, please, please tell it to me again! It can't be too bad."

A tall man with close-cropped brown hair and wire-rimmed glasses stood from his chair and placed his hand on his chest. "Mother, you know Emily will have nightmares if you do this again. But, please, it is Christmas Eve—why don't you sit by the fire and tell her a happier story?"

"I've told it to Emily for years," she said, "and she loves it. My granddaughter has the sharpest mind of any child I know. Plus, it is true. It happened to me thirty-six years ago, Marcus."

Emily colored and looked at the floor.

"Fine, just be gentle with her, ok?" He said, "I'm going to the store to pick up a few last-minute things."

"I'll be here, dear."

Grandma tilted a brown jar and poured some liquid into a blue and white striped mug with a brown handle.

"What's this?" Emily asked.

"Hot chocolate."

"But I don't want any."

"Drink some. Have a little fun. It's Christmas Eve."

"No, I don't want any."

"Oh, alright." The woman sighed and set the mug down on the counter. "You don't have to drink it."

The woman sat down in her chair again and looked at the fire.

"The story is true, Emily. It was a nightmare, but it happened. I was only twenty-one years old. Not much older than you are."

Grandma stood up and looked through the window outside. The snow was falling.

YULETIDE INVASION

"It was Christmas Eve, the first real snow of that winter. A blizzard blew into our little town, and it was a real bad one."

Emily stared at her Grandma in silence. When Grandma noticed Emily's smile, she returned it.

"The snow was thick—you couldn't see the street from our house, and the streetlights couldn't even be seen. It was just snow and darkness—and the wind."

"It was a long time ago, Grandma?"

"Yes, it was." Grandma looked into the fire and took a deep breath.

"Tell the story, Grandma."

"You always ask me to tell it on Christmas Eve."

"I know." She looked out the window again. "Look Grandma it's snowing. Please, Grandma?"

"Promise me you won't get too scared, Emily? Your father will be angry with me if you cry."

Emily closed her eyes and thought for a moment. Then, "I promise," she said.

Grandma smiled and nodded. "That's my girl."

Emily jumped up and smiled. "You were a badass Grandma!"

"You shouldn't talk like that, Emily."

"I'm sorry," Emily said. "But you were, weren't you?"

"I don't know if I was or not. I was young—the memories are a little fuzzy."

Emily hopped around excitedly. She wanted to hear the story so badly that she clapped her hands and spun in circles, making her long brown hair fly around her head.

"Alright, alright," Grandma said as she tapped Emily's bare foot with her slipper. "I'll tell you, but you have to sit back down. Are you going to sit down?"

Emily sat down on the edge of the couch.

"What happened next?" Emily was quiet for a moment. "People died, didn't they?" she said, her voice small and afraid. Grandma's eyes narrowed to slits as she squeezed her glasses with her thumb and index finger, the bones in her hands protruding.

"Yes, people died. It was a bad time."

"It's a sad story, Grandma," Emily said.

"Yes, it is, but it's better now."

"Better?"

"Yes, it's better that I can tell you the story, so the people who died won't have been forgotten."

"I'll never forget them," Emily said. "I'll never forget you either, Grandma."

"No, you won't forget. That's why I tell the story—so that one day, you'll tell this story to your children and then to your grandchildren."

Emily nodded.

"Now, are you ready for the story to begin?"

"Yes, I am ready Grandma!"

"Ok, here we go..."

Two

The Blizzard

Gloria was late for her night shift at the RJ's Super Market & Convenience Store. Her boss was going to be furious. She cursed under her breath as she drove through the snowstorm. She almost rear-ended the pickup truck in front of her, and the road was so slippery that she nearly lost control of the car twice. Finally, when the storm threatened to sweep her off the road into a ditch, she pulled in and parked.

The sign was peeling. A cracked, jagged, chipped S appeared in the middle of the white letters. The bottom half of the letter was faded entirely, and a small strip of blue duct tape held it in place.

YULETIDE INVASION

She bundled up and left the car, stepping out into the whipping snow as she made her way to the store to begin her shift.

Gloria rolled the door open and stepped inside. She felt oddly compelled to stop and look at all the dangling toys, their tinsel garlands sparkling in the store lights. The jingle bells on the door made a nice little tinkling noise as she shut it behind her. She raised an eyebrow at the overabundance of Christmas decorations but couldn't resist one last look. Then she sighed and walked to the back office to punch in for her shift.

A short man in tight pants and a button-down shirt, with a pencil-thin mustache and tortoiseshell academic-style glasses, was perched on a plastic chair and smoking, facing away from Gloria. She removed her coat and clocked in.

"Hello, Gloria. Since it is Christmas Eve, I will pay you for the time you missed being late. I know the weather is bad, and I appreciate you working tonight," he said.

Gloria stammered, "Well, uh, thank you, Mr. Jackson. I'm sorry that you had to stay longer."

"You have nothing to be sorry for. I am a forgiving man. I can understand why you're late. Just do not let it happen again," he said, tapping the cigarette with his thumb.

Gloria looked away, "Y-Y–you are too generous, sir. I won't let it happen again."

"I am leaving for the night. Sam is on duty tonight as well. He is stocking the shelves. Ensure you lock up and set the alarms tonight when you leave. The store closes at 2 AM," he said, pulling the cigarette out of his mouth and flicking it into the wastebasket in the corner.

"Will do, Mr. Jackson," Gloria said, walking out of the office.

She walked to the register and set her clipboard on the counter. 'Sleigh Ride' blared out of speakers. She hated Christmas songs. She opened the cash register and began counting out the money for the night. She had only taken the shift because it paid time and a half, and she worried her rent would be late.

"Merry Christmas, Gloria," a familiar voice behind her said.

Quickly turning around, Gloria answered, "Oh, hi Sam. How are you?"

Gloria took her hand and brushed back her curly blonde hair, pulling it from its elastic band.

He was a tall, thin boy with medium-length dark hair that fell in perfect waves at the bottom of a well-pressed shirt. He wore a bright blue button-down with a name tag. His hands were tucked into the pockets of his jeans.

"There haven't been many people tonight with that snow and it being Christmas Eve. So it is just us suckers stuck here," Sam laughed.

Mr. Jackson walked toward the door to leave for the night. "Don't forget to close the doors and set the alarms, Gloria," he said as he walked out.

"We know, we know, we know," Sam said, waving his hand in front of Gloria.

The store was nearly empty. A heavy-set woman with a gray bun stood — arms folded, feet apart, lips pursed — in the checkout line. Gloria cashed out the woman's items and said, "Merry Christmas," as she handed her the receipt.

"Merry Christmas," she replied, taking the receipt and picking up her bag to leave. The bells of the large Catholic Church to the east rang out, signaling the start of the first Christmas Eve service. She opened the door.

"I wonder why Mr. Jackson didn't close the place with this snowstorm," Sam said as he walked up to the register.

Gloria shook her head. "You don't understand. This guy is a dick. He doesn't ever close on Christmas Eve. I only took this shift so I could pay rent."

Sam crumpled up his empty chip bag, tossing it into the trash.

"It's just my mom and me this year for Christmas. Dad left my mom for what she said was a younger woman. So she's sitting at home alone on Christmas Eve, probably getting drunk. All I want is to be with my family. I hate my dad for doing this to my mom," Sam said. His lower lip quivered as he fought back the tears.

Gloria wrapped her arms around him and smoothed his hair. "It will be okay."

"I'm not sure. I don't think she will be okay," he replied.

'Listen...," Gloria stopped and shook her head, "I know you're having a terrible year. Come back here. I have something to show you in the employee lounge that may cheer you up," Gloria said, leading Sam back to the lounge.

Gloria bent down and pulled her purse from her locker. She fished around in it and pulled out a small package. She handed him the small gift.

"You didn't have to do this," he said, looking at the small box wrapped in blue paper.

"Yes, I did. I'll be right back. Stay here," she said, walking out the door.

A few minutes later, she returned, carrying a liquor bottle.

"Let's have some fun tonight. Let's get a little drunk," Gloria said, unscrewing the cap on the bottle.

"I can't, Gloria. I'm only nineteen," Sam said, looking at the bottle of alcohol in her hand.

YULETIDE INVASION

Gloria laughed, "Don't freak out on me, Sam," she said, taking a swig from the bottle.

"I don't know. It's just not my style," he replied.

"Come on, Sam. It's Christmas Eve. We can't spend Christmas Eve at work and not at least have a little fun," she said, taking another drink.

"I don't know. I was looking forward to tonight. I was going to sit on my couch with a blanket and watch 'It's a Wonderful Life' with my mom before I got called into work," he said, looking at the bottle in her hand.

"Well, live a little, Sam. Let's have some fun. We can at least have a little drink. It will help us get through the night," she said, handing the bottle to Sam.

Sam snatched the bottle out of her hand, took a large gulp, and coughed.

"Wow, that's powerful stuff," he said, handing her back the bottle.

Gloria took another swig and handed the bottle back to Sam. "See? I told you it would be good."

Sam took another drink and handed the bottle back to Gloria.

"I'm not feeling anything yet," Sam said, swiping the backs of his hands over his mouth.

"Oh, but you will," Gloria said, handing him back the bottle.

Sam took a long drink from the bottle as Gloria pulled out some cigarettes. She lit one, took a drag, and then held it out for Sam to take a drag.

"You know I can't do this. I've never even had a cigarette before," Sam said as he took the cigarette from her and took a long drag.

Gloria laughed as Sam coughed. "You look silly."

"It tastes terrible," he said, coughing. He handed Gloria back the cigarette.

"So, why are you always alone? I've only seen you with that guy Eddie. Are you gay?" she asked with a chuckle.

"No, I'm not gay," Sam replied.

Gloria took the bottle back from Sam and took a drink.

"Is it because you're ugly?" Gloria asked.

Sam looked at her, paused, and then started laughing.

"That's not nice. Besides, you're the most beautiful woman I've ever seen," Sam replied.

"Oh, I'm sure that's a lie," Gloria said, taking a sip.

"No, it's not. I've seen enough to know you are the most beautiful woman I've ever seen," he replied.

"I bet you say that to all the girls," she said, taking a long drag from her cigarette.

"What if someone comes into the store while we drink, Gloria? I don't want to get fired."

"Man, have you seen that weather out there? They say it is now a blizzard. Nobody is going to come to this stupid place tonight. They're safe and doing their family Christmas shit. So why shouldn't we have a little fun? Come on, Sam, loosen up and have a little fun with me. I just want to veg out," Gloria said, taking another swig from the bottle.

Sam took another long drink of the scotch and handed the bottle back to Gloria. "This stuff is amazing. It is kicking in. I am starting to feel pretty drunk."

"I told you so," she replied.

Sam stirred from his chair as Gloria drank and clicked the light switch. The music was louder. 'Run Rudolph' blared throughout the tiny space.

"You know, Gloria, you really are the most beautiful woman I've ever seen," he said, stumbling slightly.

"And you're a complete mess," she replied.

"You think so? I'm a mess?" Sam asked, stepping closer to Gloria.

"Oh, you are a complete mess. Besides, I have a boyfriend," Gloria said, moving away from him.

Sam stepped closer. "Ah, but what if you weren't dating him?"

"You don't play fair, Sam. You are drunk." Gloria said as she took a long drink.

"You are right. I am having fun. I'm drunk. I can't believe I have never done this before. I feel...."

Sam suddenly lurched toward the garbage can, pulled the lid off, and puked.

"Oh God, I'm sorry," he said as he pressed his hand against the wall to steady himself.

"Uh, you shouldn't have done that," she said, moving away from him.

"Don't worry, I'll clean it up," Sam said as he stumbled toward the garbage can, spitting and wracking his body.

Gloria laughed, "You can't do that, chill. I'll get it. Just let me go get a mop. I'll be right back."

"Oh God, I'm sorry," Sam said again, his back to Gloria.

Gloria walked back toward the supply room to get a mop when the DING DONG sound of someone entering the store went off. She looked up at the door, and nobody was there.

"That's weird," she said as she grabbed the mop.

Sam followed her toward the room, looking embarrassed.

"Did I hear someone come in?" he asked.

"Yeah, but it went off. I looked up. Nobody was there," she said.

"That's weird. I wonder who it was," Sam said, looking out the window.

YULETIDE INVASION

"Are you feeling better, or need to puke some more?"

"I'm fine," Sam said, sitting at the cash register.

"I am going to clean up your gnarly mess." Gloria started walking back to the garbage can with the mop.

"Okay, sorry. How embarrassing."

Sam stared out the windows, watching snow collect on the sill. Gloria bustled around behind him, cleaning up the mess. He heard her muttering under her breath and was grateful she was ignoring him.

He walked over, ran his hand along the window, and watched his wavy reflection. He could have sworn he saw a shadow dart across the glass and then vanish, but he figured it was because he was drunk.

Gloria came back to the register, pinching her nose.

"Well, that sucked. I cleaned up your puke. Gag me with a spoon!"

"Thanks. I hope I didn't ruin your night too much," he replied.

"Don't worry about it. I'm still having a good time, and now that I am getting a little tipsy, I might unwrap one of these gifts."

"Oh, you shouldn't do that," Sam said.

"Why not? I'm the one who got them for us," she replied.

"Yeah, but I never open gifts on Christmas Eve. We never even really sang carols."

Gloria leaned over, slapped her knee, and laughed, "Oh, come on, you sing carols?"

"It was a corny tradition my family did before my dad left my mom. We all had a nice little Christmas party, and everyone sang a song about Christmas to the whole family."

"How nice," Gloria said.

"Yeah, it was nice. I miss it."

"Well, why don't we do it now?" she asked.

"Do you really want to?"

"Sure. It sounds corny as hell, but I am game. What do you think we should sing first?" Gloria asked.

"Well, first, we should sing a little song that my family always sang together," said Sam.

"What is it?"

Sam looked embarrassed. 'The First Noel,' he answered.

"Oh shit, that is corny. Alright, let's sing it, Sam. It's Christmas, and who cares if it's corny," she replied.

"Okay, let's start," Sam said. "The first Noel the angel said was to certain poor shepherds in fields as they lay..."

Suddenly, the ceiling shook. The lights dimmed and then went out completely. Then, from the rear of the shop, a loud crashing sound filled the room. Next, there was a loud pop from the power box behind the register.

"What the hell!" Gloria yelled.

"The storm must have blown out the power. But what was that loud noise?" Sam asked.

Gloria pointed to the ceiling. "That's probably one of the heating systems."

"Why would the heat make that noise?" he asked.

"Now, what do we do? Do we call Mr. Jackson?" She asked, throwing her arms into the air.

They heard another crash and a few pops. Then there was a brief silence, followed by another bang and a crescendo of breaking glass.

"I can't see a fucking thing!" Gloria yelled.

A scraping sound was heading in their direction, and then a crash to their right.

"Jesus, what is that? What is all that noise?" Sam asked.

The scratching drew closer, like claws scraping the floor. Sam could see nothing. He swung his arms in the dark and felt whatever was coming toward him. It brushed against his arms.

"Gloria, there is something right by me. It brushed up against me!"

"I can't see a fucking thing, Sam."

When the lights came back on, Gloria could see the outline of a dog circling her, wagging its tail. She looked down and saw its fur pressed against her leg, leaving a wet mark on her jeans.

"Hey," she said as she kneeled and scratched behind its ear. "Where the hell did you come from?" Gloria asked.

The dog wagged its tail and licked its lips as it padded to the cash register.

"What is it doing?" Sam asked.

"Fuck if I know. Maybe it's afraid of the dark," she said.

Sam said, "Hey, boy," in a voice high and squeaky with forced friendliness. The dog growled, staring at the door with eyes narrowed to slits. Its lips lifted over its teeth.

And then he heard it—soft padding in the distance. Closer, closer, closer. It was getting louder. Something was coming up behind him. He turned around in time to see something move.

THREE

The Accident

GABE GRIPPED THE STEERING wheel of his Ford Pinto and stared at the snow churning against the windshield. The wipers beat a steady drumbeat and swiped at the snowflakes that made it past, but he could barely see more than two feet in front of him. To take his mind off the storm, he tried to imagine how his girlfriend Jamie would look after six months apart. He imagined her standing at the doorway with her hands on her hips, hair falling in loose waves around her shoulders, and her eyes scrunched. Gabe shook his head. If he had kept going south, he would have eventually reached Buffalo by now.

Once, Gabe had driven to a hockey game with some friends in Buffalo. Unfortunately, he got stuck in a snowstorm on the way home. It had taken him almost four hours to get back to Rochester, and the entire drive, he'd watched the snow pile up on the side of the highway.

Gabe passed by a car that was upside down in the ditch. He slowed down and got out. He peered at the headlights shining back at him. The car was a Honda, crumpled on one side and half-buried in the snow. He could see Christmas gifts spilling out of the trunk, which had been torn open; the right side window was smashed, too. Stains of blood were on the passenger seat.

Gabe rummaged through the back seat and found a deck of cards. "Instructions for use" was scrawled on the top of the box. He shuffled through the cards, glanced at an image of a white-bearded man pointing, and tossed it back.

He looked at the driver's seat. A thick smear of blood covered the wheel. The keys were still inside, and the radio played 'Christmas (Baby Please Come Home).' In the passenger seat, the force of the crash had smashed a giant plastic snowman's head sideways. Two sets of footprints led away from the car, but they stopped after about ten feet.

"That is weird," Gabe said out loud.

Gabe trudged back to his car and pulled back onto the highway. But unfortunately, his gas tank was on "E," and he desperately needed to find an exit.

YULETIDE INVASION

Gabe never drove fast on the ice over the winter, but it was dark, and he felt vulnerable. So he was speeding, making up for the time he'd lost.

A circular beam of light shot over the road, illuminating an ominous metallic shape blocking his path. He looked away for a split second, and the car jerked to the right. He slammed on the brakes but wobbled off the road, plowing into a snow-filled ditch. The car's horn came alive, filling the air with a shrill sound.

"Shit!" he shouted.

Gabe stepped out of his car and sank ankle-deep in the snow. The snow had changed from whirling flurries into heavy piles that swirled around his knees like clouds.

He stumbled along the road and turned his head to the left. He made out the word "DINER" in blue neon. He pushed open the door, stomped snow from his boots, and entered a small restaurant covered with Christmas decorations. The smell of fried onions drifted into his nose as he stood beneath an artificial Christmas tree decorated with blinking lights.

A large man with dark, shiny eyes leaned over the counter. A neon-green vest covered his barrel chest. He wore a black cap with red stitching.

"This is quite a storm," he said as he nodded at Gabe. "Welcome. Come on in and get warmed up."

"I would love something hot to drink," said Gabe.

"Coming right up. Hope coffee is ok."

"Sure," Gabe smiled.

"This storm has gone on for quite a while. The snow is supposed to keep falling till tomorrow morning."

"You're kidding me."

"No sir, I ain't."

The man leaned in close to shake Gabe's hand and grinned, revealing a broken tooth on the left side and two other teeth stained yellow from smoking. His eyes shined with brightness.

"I do the cookin', and my wife, Barbara, she's here too. We own this place; it's a little joint but a good one." He pointed to a small wooden chair and table across the room. "Please, have a seat."

Geno headed toward a skinny metal stand that held a black-and-white television and pushed it aside, making space for the glasses. A remote control and an old coin candy machine sat on the shelf next to a newspaper and reading glasses.

Geno looked from side to side, examined Gabe for a moment, and then shrugged. "Ya know, I rarely ask this," he said. "You don't judge me for asking?"

Gabe swiveled around in his chair and rested his arms—his biceps bulging—on the back of the chair. His brown eyes narrowed as he folded them across his chest. "What's your question?"

"So what brings an out-of-towner like you to this little town?" Geno asked.

"I was on my way to Buffalo to spend Christmas with my girlfriend," he explained. "I'm a Manhattan insurance sales agent. My car jackknifed into a ditch."

Geno laughed, "Man, you got yourself way out in the sticks. Sorry to hear that."

Gabe paid for his drink and sat back in his chair. "Maybe so. It's not where I want to be at the moment."

Geno winked at him. "I gather you're in a little trouble, too, huh?"

"What makes you ask that?" Gabe replied.

"It's like I told my wife, Barbara. We filled this town with people trying to escape their troubles."

"I'm no exception," Gabe said.

Geno nodded and turned to a newspaper. "We gave time off to our staff. To let them spend time with their families, you know."

"I assumed that," Gabe replied.

"Alright, I'm a talker, so here's my thing. This whole Christmas thing, it doesn't matter."

"What do you mean?"

"Look everywhere around you, and you see people who are hurting. But, unfortunately, some of them are hurting bad."

"I am not sure that I am following you."

"I mean, Christmas ain't about the presents. It's about people. It's about helping other people. So I will not let the holiday season pass without helping some folks."

Gabe twirled a fork in his fingers. "Well, that is nice of you. You don't feel like Christmas is important?"

Geno laughed. "I feel like Christmas is a lie. It's a story, a terrible story. It's all greed. Christmas makes no sense anymore. It is all about the gifts now."

"I get it. I do."

Geno leaned in, raising his voice over the sound of the radio. "People out there do not get a Christmas this year. So I will be that person who ensures that at least one person gets a Christmas."

"It's all about what's inside you," Gabe said.

"Listen," Geno said. "You are right. I am not a religious man, but I still believe in something. I believe in family."

Gabe smiled and clapped his hands. "Me too."

"You know what? A while back, I came across an article that said at least one in twelve people in the United States are not getting a Christmas this year. That is a lot of people."

"Yes, it is."

"Listen, man, sorry if I am bummin' you out. I get a little carried away sometimes," Geno said with laughter.

"You know," Gabe said. "I had a friend once who said, 'you can't save their world, but you can save their day.'"

"That is a smart friend, my brother," Geno said.

Gabe sipped his drink. "Hey, do you guys have a phone, so I can call my girlfriend? She is probably worried about me," Gabe said.

Geno pointed to a green rotary telephone on the counter next to a pile of newspapers and a red plastic cup.

"Thanks," Gabe said.

He dialed the number and waited for his girlfriend to answer.

"Hello, is this Michele?"

"Yes, this is. Gabe, Is that you? I was so worried. Why didn't you call me? Please, tell me you're okay."

"I'm okay. I had a minor accident and may not get to Buffalo until tomorrow. There is a blizzard here. I am in Elview."

"Oh, man, that is three hours away in good weather. Are you ok? Are you hurt? What happened?"

He frowned. "I'm sorry I didn't call sooner—just a little sleep-deprived. I'm fine. I'll be there as quickly as possible, I'll be back. Sorry to worry about you. I love you."

"Don't worry about me. Being in the middle of nowhere is hard, but never mind. I'll be fine. I love you too."

"Alright, Merry Christmas, baby."

"Merry Christmas, love you too."

Gabe hung up the phone and turned to Geno. "Thanks," he said.

"No problem," Geno replied.

Geno poured Gabe another cup of hot coffee and handed it to him. Gabe thanked him, and they sat in silence.

Four

The Newcomers

THE DINER DOOR FLUNG open, and a gust of snowy air rushed in, mingling with the scent of body odor drifting, cloying and heavy across the room. In the doorway stood a man who looked into Gabe's eyes. He wore a faded black leather jacket, oversize pants, and a shirt with a turned-up collar. Beside him stood a girl, who—despite the overalls and baseball cap she wore—had the first hint of a plump pregnancy in her belly. A brown and white dog with snowflakes stuck to its coat walked through the diner's doorway and wagged its tail.

"Merry Christmas. Come in and get warmed up folks," Geno said with a smile.

A gray-haired woman emerged from the kitchen into the dining room. "You guys hungry? I am Barbara," she asked as she extended her hand to the couple.

"Wow, okay. I am starving. I'm Frank, and this is Leah, my fiancé," he said, making a circular gesture at Leah.

"Pleased to meet you," Gabe extended his hand, and Frank sloppily shook it.

Leah looked down at her feet and batted her eyelashes and smiled. "This is Bruno," she said. "He's our dog. Hope that is ok for him to be here tonight."

Frank took Leah's coat and hung it up on a peg. He motioned to the table. "Mind if we sit over there?"

Geno nodded at the couple and said, "Sure thing. I'll bring you some menus. Your dog is welcome here tonight."

On the radio, the newsman was talking about the blizzard. "Look at this storm currently moving east from the lakes," he said. "It's already hit us over four feet in Western New York. So people should stay indoors tonight; don't leave. This blizzard is the worst storm to hit us since 1977! There is a travel advisory in every county."

The music started again, and Bing Crosby was singing about a White Christmas.

Suddenly, the dog stood frozen and quivering, its fur standing on end, its ears and eyes blazing with anger, its mouth agape, staring at the door. He raised the tip of his tail.

Frank approached the dog. "Bruno, what has gotten into you, buddy?" The dog whined and rolled his eyes. Frank reached out to pet it but fell back with his hand in his hair. The dog growled and lunged at Frank. Again, Frank fell, and the dog loped at the door.

Geno walked up, a look of concern on his face, "Your dog usually does this to y'all?"

"Never," Leah said. She was wringing her hands.

Gabe looked at Geno, who shrugged and went back to the kitchen.

"What is this dog's problem?" Frank asked.

"Maybe he needs to use the bathroom," Leah said.

Frank bent over to put a leash on Bruno and the dog snapped at his hand, snarling and spittle frothing at the corners of his mouth. "Why is he biting me?" Frank asked.

The radio suddenly went dead. The lights flickered, dimmed, then went out completely.

Outside, a flash of lightning split the sky and surrounded the diner in a flickering glow. A long, dark shape passed outside the window, casting a giant shadow on the floor.

"What the hell was that?" Gabe said while looking around the room.

"Did you see that?" Leah asked.

"Seen what?" Barbara asked.

"Something outside," Leah replied.

"Probably someone walking into the store next door, guys," Geno said. He was wiping the tables.

"Yeah, well, I saw something else," Frank said.

The radio halted during Springsteen's 'Santa Claus is Coming to Town'. The tree, a bauble and tinsel-studded one, blinked out in the restaurant's center. At one point, only an array of Christmas tree lights remained in the room. Then all the lights went out: the neon signs, the colored lights, and even the candles. The restaurant was in total darkness.

"Shit! What the fuck is going on?" Geno said.

"I can't see a damn thing now," Frank responded.

"Must be the storm," Barbara said. She could hear Frank walking around and felt his hand touch her shoulder. She didn't respond—she was focused on the dog, which had been growling.

"It's ok, Bruno," Leah said as she reached down to pet the dog, but it simply issued a low growl at her.

Gabe asked Geno if he had a generator.

"Yeah, yeah, I have one. Let me get it. It is in the shed out back where I keep the freezer," Geno said, doing a mental inventory.

Barbara reached around the counter, felt her way to the flashlight, and handed it to Geno. "Be careful," she said. "It is terrible out there.

"I will, baby," Geno gave her a kiss and turned to the back door. The moonlight illuminated his startled face as he walked through the snow drifts and into the darkness.

"I hope this will work at least for some heat," Leah said.

Geno's blood-curdling scream was the only sound that ripped through the night.

Five

The Shed

WHEN THE LIGHTS CAME back, everyone had a look of panic. The radio was blaring, 'Feliz Navidad.'

Gabe ran to the door. "Sounds like something happened to Geno. I am going to go out and check on him."

"I'll go with you," Barbara said. She had a flashlight in her hand.

The two of them walked out the door and down the steps. They stepped into the snow and looked up. The sky above was a flurry of conflicting lights, with blue, yellow, red, and white streaks. "Oh my God," Barbara said.

The shed door was ajar, and the snow had a streak of blood leading inside. The interior of the shed was a dark, solid mass. The single beam of the flashlight cut a thick swathe of light into the dark, and the light touched Geno on the floor.

His body was contorted, one leg twisted at an unnatural angle and the other hanging loose. The foot on his dangling leg pointed to the bottom of the door. They cut his body open from his neck to his groin. Organs were strewn all around the shed.

Barbara screamed and dropped to her knees, and her flashlight rolled away.

"Oh my God," she said.

Gabe backed away, his hand over his mouth and nose, his eyes unable to focus. He fell over into the snow and he was still.

She was pounding at the snow with her fists, shaking her whole body and sobbing.

"We need to get back inside now," Gabe said firmly.

He stood back up and reached out and took Barbara's hand and helped her up. She followed him through the back door and into the diner again. When they were both safely inside, Gabe locked it.

They stood in silence for a long moment. Barbara's eyes were red, and her mascara was smeared. She sniffed and cried again.

Leah was shaking and stammered up to Gabe. "What happened?"

"Somebody killed Geno," Barbara said.

"What?" Leah said.

"They cut him up and left him out here like he was an animal," Barbara said.

"What are we going to do?" Leah asked.

"We have to get help," Barbara said between tears. Leah was circling the room in a panic.

They were all in the dining room, peering out the windows to the shed.

Something leaped out of sight, and a shadowy figure appeared in the shed's doorway.

"There is a killer still out there. We need to call the police now!" Gabe said.

Barbara was in shock. She was so pale she looked ghostly, and her lips moved, making no sounds. The dog barked haphazardly at the door, jumping to one side and the other. The tail wagged, but the eyes remained locked on the left door.

Gabe walked over to the phone. He picked up the receiver and sighed, "Great, the line is dead."

A loud slam at the rear door made everyone jump.

Barbara's eyes were wild. Finally, she whispered, "What is that?"

Bruno leaped at the door, sinking his teeth into its handle. His eyes glowed like embers, and he let out a low, menacing growl, which swelled into a hungry, furious howl of anger.

She could make out the shape of a figure standing outside in the heavy snowfall. But an inhuman voice that sounded like it was gargling from the bottom of a well shouted, "Put me out of my misery, Barbara."

"No!" Gabe shouted. Frank held Barbara back from the door, his hands on her shoulders.

"It's Geno," said Barbara. She reached for the doorknob, her manic movements only barely contained.

The door slammed again. "Barbara!" the voice said. "I'm fine. Come here my darling."

There was a crash, and the ripped-out window on the door showed a slim arm reaching into the diner. The dog snarled and leaped toward it, fangs bared.

Foreboding crept through the diner as the door swung open, and a figure stumbled through. Geno's blood coated its face and chest, and behind it, all of his innards trailed out of the gash in his abdomen.

Barbara tried to pull Frank and Gabe away, but couldn't. Leah cowered in the corner. The dog's snarling snout snapped at her flailing arms, but the terrible choking noises came from Geno. His blood spattered the walls and spread a wide swath across the floorboards. He arched his back as his throat gave one final gurgling sound, then lay still in a growing pool of blood.

The dog ran out the door, bounded through the snow, and charged into the night, barking furiously.

Six

The Intruder

"There is something in here with us," Gloria whispered.

Sam looked like he was going to throw up again. She could hear his heartbeat, his chest heaving up and down. He turned his head toward her, and his eyes looked frantic, scared shitless.

"I'm scared Gloria," Sam said.

"Listen, Sam. I will get the shotgun that Mr. Jackson keeps for safety behind the cash register."

"No! Are you crazy?" Sam asked.

"No, you are crazy! Do you want to sit here while whatever is in here kills us?"

"No. But do you know how to use it? What if it isn't here to kill us?"

"I've never shot a gun before, but I am going to learn," she said.

Sam touched Gloria's cheek. "Please be careful."

"I will," she said. She squeezed Sam's hand, stood, and started walking into the darkness.

A growl rose and fell through the murk. Then a high-pitched whine joined in. A gurgling whimper cut through the silence a few feet in front of Gloria. She focused on the noise and found her way to the register by touch. Another whine joined in, followed by deep, guttural groans mixed with snarls.

Gloria felt around for the drawer in the dark and discovered a small latch, which she jiggled with her thumb. She reached behind the register and pulled on it, but it didn't give. Then she tried to squirm behind the cash register, but it wedged too tightly around her body in the space between the desk and a wall.

Gloria heard a mournful, hollow moan that was more felt than heard. It seemed to emanate from the inky blackness around her. She pivoted on her heel and turned around, but she couldn't see anything but the vague, oblong shape of the doorway. Her muscles tightened as though freezing in place. She wanted to get out of there and tried to turn and run back to Sam.

She ran her hands over the counter. The cold steel of the 12 gauge Browning bumped up against her knuckles. She wrapped her fingers around the butt of the gun. She checked the safety and ran her hand over the metal.

A warm, wet exhale slid down her shoulder. Then her fingers probed in the darkness. It was a heavy, contented sound laced with menace. She tried to scream, but no sound came out.

Suddenly, she saw the dog dash past her and heard growling and signs of a struggle. Then there was a loud thump and a low whine. Then, a wet thump hit the floor, and Gloria heard slobbering.

She shifted her weight and gritted her teeth. A warm shudder ran down her spine, and her body jerked.

The figure was a half-human, half-insect creature. Its skin was the soft, hardened shell of an insect that glistened as if covered in slime, and its limbs were a fluid mass of writhing tendrils. As the dog lunged at it, the monster tumbled back and stood up uncertainly. It had many writhing tendrils for a head, large black multifaceted eyes, and four thin insectoid appendages sprouting from its shoulders.

"What the hell are you? Where did you come from?" Gloria asked. She stared at the creature, stunned by its squirming, boneless body. It was eight feet tall and had long, thin arms that hung down to the floor. A mass of writhing tentacles shot out of the center when it looked at her.

The creature snarled at her and swatted the shotgun away with one of its long, spindly arms. The gun skittered across the floor, and Gloria stumbled backward.

Footsteps approached from behind her. "Gloria, get back!" Sam said.

"What the hell are you doing in here? I told you to stay put," she said.

Sam stepped in front of Gloria with a pipe raised over his head. The creature whipped around and punched him in the jaw, doubling him. It held him against the floor with one hand, then swung its arm back towards Gloria's throat. She fell back, and its legs entwined with hers.

She stomped on the twisted ankle, and it let go, howling and rolling on the ground with a dark gash in its purple skin. A viscous fluid, like thinned-out black blood, dripped from its mouth.

The dog nipped at the creature's calf, but it swatted the dog away with one of its powerful legs, sending it sliding across the floor. The dog turned and lunged for the creature's arm, but it threw its arm down just in time, and the dog's teeth sank into its elbow. Then, with a snarl, the creature twisted and slammed the dog to the floor. It raised one foot high in the air and then brought it down on the dog's midsection, knocking the wind out. The dog yelped, rolled over once, and scampered to safety.

The creature turned its attention back to Gloria, holding the gun with both hands. Gloria steadied the grip on the gun, pressing it into her right shoulder. Her hands trembled as she held it.

"Come on, you son of a bitch!" she shouted.

Sam lunged at the creature.

Gloria shouted, "No! Sam, no!"

The creature raised its left leg and swung in a wide semicircle, slicing the air just centimeters above Sam's head, then drove a black-nailed foot into Sam's chest. He fell onto the floor and clutched his sternum in agony.

She tried to scramble out of reach, but the thing's legs were longer than hers. It opened its mouth and chittered as it fell on her, gouging her arm with its claws.

Gloria scrambled for the shotgun and grabbed it. Another hand wrapped around her ankle, and she jerked her leg back. She crawled on all fours back to the end of the counter and kicked out blindly. Her foot struck a baggy cheek, and the creature groaned.

She grabbed the gun, stood up, and fired. Unfortunately, the recoil knocked her back, and she fell.

As soon as the bullet hit, the creature's head flew apart, like a watermelon struck by a baseball bat, and white, syrupy brain matter burst out in all directions.

Sam crawled over to the shotgun and picked it up. He stood up and tossed it to Gloria. "What the hell was that thing?"

"Something straight out of hell, Sam. I want to get out of here now," she said.

"Yeah, me too."

Sam walked past Gloria towards the door.

"Sam, wait," she said.

He paused in the doorway. "What is it?"

"We should call the police."

Sam walked over to the phone by the register and picked it up.

"The line is dead," he said.

The dog suddenly appeared, limping but alive, in the doorway.

"Hey there, buddy. Glad to see you survived." Gloria bent over and stroked the dog's fur.

"Well, we should see if anyone is at the diner next door. Maybe their phone works."

The dog stood on his hind legs and put his paws on Sam's arm. Sam locked eyes with the dog and smiled.

"Let's go," he said. They stepped into a whirling vortex of white. Snow crunched beneath their feet as they trudged toward the yellow glow of warm light from the diner.

Seven

What Used To Be Geno

Geno's back split open, and a pair of legs dangling from his rib cage like dead branches from a tree.

As Leah stared at him, he grew closer, his eyes wild and his jaw missing. He moved with a strange scuttling motion. His legs bent unnaturally backward, balanced on fingers that tapped against the floor as he moved. His body looked ragged and torn.

"The cellar! The cellar!" Gabe yelled.

Gabe picked up his overturned chair, gritted his teeth, and flipped it over before slamming it into the creature's

YULETIDE INVASION

back. It burst through the air, shattering and knocking it against the wall with a loud thud.

They ran into the basement while Frank slammed the door behind them, latching it.

The basement growled and shook. The walls, along with the door and stairs, trembled as if someone was trying to get through from outside. And then there were the sounds of glass shattering and plates shattering. There was a single light bulb in the ceiling socket, but the cord had come loose, and the bulb was hanging out of its socket, swaying back and forth with each movement. The cellar smelled musty and damp like it never got enough air.

They crouched against the wall in the corner and listened to the sounds of clawing, growling, and footfalls up above. Barbara was crying and shuddering.

Frank gripped Barbara's hand tightly on gently put his other hand over her mouth, "Shhh."

Above them, they could hear shrieks and bangs on the door as the thing that was no longer Geno tried to get through.

"What are we going to do?" Leah asked.

"We're going to keep quiet," Frank answered.

The door above them buckled and cracked from an unseen force, the wood shards raining down on them. Gabe felt his arms break out in gooseflesh, and suddenly he was freezing, his teeth clattering. His heart was thudding behind his rib cage.

Gabe flicked on his flashlight and looked around the room, searching for something to defend themselves with. In one corner of the room, he found an old shovel leaning against the wall. He picked it up and handed it to Leah. Then, searching around under the messy piles of papers stacked on top of an old desk, he found an old baseball bat. He gave it to Frank.

Suddenly dust and grit fell from the ceiling, and the floorboards creaked and groaned from footsteps. Two gunshots rang out in quick succession, each one like thunder echoing off of the cellar walls.

Gabe tiptoed up the stairs, his heart racing. Suddenly ahead, he heard soft footsteps and a swishing sound. He paused, crouched, and listened; the footsteps stopped. He crept carefully up the stairs and peeked under the door landing.

A knock came on the door, and Gabe froze. He held a finger to his lips, and the others nodded silently.

"Hello?" a woman's voice called through the door.

YULETIDE INVASION

Gabe kicked in the door, splintering the wood around the lock, and stumbled into the room. He was holding a hammer, and his eyes widened as he saw a young woman with curly blonde hair covered in blood holding a shotgun. Behind her was a young man with wild eyes and a dark, crescent-shaped wound on his forehead.

Gloria shook their hands and muttered something about a good goddamn thing. "Well, what do you know?" she said. "Think I did a number on it. Eh?"

"Sure looks like it to me," Gabe answered.

The blood-smeared dining room walls and floor were sprayed with gore, like graffiti. Gabe felt sick to his stomach.

The young man looked at Gabe. "Hey, I'm Sam. I think we are safe for the moment."

Barbara's jaw hung open, and she took a few steps toward Gabe, her body trembling. "Geno, my baby," she said. Her eyes tracked to a crater on the floor where her husband had been just moments before. Big chunks of him were smoking in the hole. Leah held her arm, trying to support her.

"He was like us," she said through her sobs.

"We need to find a way of calling the police," Gloria said. "We need to get out of here. And," she looked around at the others, "We to arm ourselves. I have no more ammo left. Whatever is going on, it can change people into these things."

Leah screamed, "Bruno!" as the dog came to her and licked her cheek. The dog spun in circles and howled at the door to the kitchen as if it were a dog whistle and he was answering it. Gabe bent down and gave the dog a rub on the head.

Barbara surged up the stairs, her nostrils flaring. She stopped short at the top and stared at a trail of something dark and glistening that ended in a red puddle on the floor.

Barbara couldn't look away. She stared at the body, at the thing that Geno had become. The room felt thick and warm with a broad, rich disgust that clung to her lips.

"What did it turn him into?" she asked.

She turned to Gabe, who had sunk to his knees beside the body.

"Something horrible," he answered.

"Oh God," she said, one hand over her mouth and the other on her chest. Tears streamed down her face.

They all stood in a half-circle around the body, wearing expressions of horror, sadness, and confusion.

The silence stretched out uncomfortably until Gloria finally broke it. "We killed one of these things next door before we came here to use your phone. This might be contagious."

"So, where is the phone in here?" Sam asked.

Gabe glanced at the wall and patiently said, "The phone is over there bud. But it is dead.

Sam walked over and tried the phone. He cursed under his breath. "It doesn't work."

"Do you think we can drive through this blizzard to get help? I mean, the snow is at least three feet everywhere," Gloria said.

Frank walked in circles around the group, his hands outstretched, his eyes bright. "We might make it through the snow in the truck," he said.

"We need to get to a police station," said Gloria. "The closest is about two miles from here."

"I don't know how far we'll get," said Gabe. He ran his fingers through his hair, then pulled on the ends. "It's too deep out there."

"Well, I would rather die trying. But, even if we have to walk through the snow, anything is better than staying here," said Gloria.

A deafening silence fell over the group like a heavy wool blanket. It grew tighter and tighter by the second as Gabe swallowed hard and nodded.

"I know," he said. "I'm scared too."

They all knew that they might not survive.

Eight
Looking For Help

The group headed out the door into the swirling curtain of ice and snow.

"Guys, there is no way that this thing will even make it through the snow," Sam said. "Even if we clear the snow, the power will be out, and it will get stuck in the middle of the blizzard."

"We need to weight down the truck as much as we can for better traction," Frank said.

Gloria turned to Sam. "Hey, you impressed me back there."

"Thanks. Sorry that I went all puke-face on you," Sam said. "I have eaten nothing in days. That booze hit me hard."

"Well, it was brave of you to help to protect me," Gloria said.

"Eh, I was doing what I had to. Plus, you are the hottest chick I know," Sam answered.

Gabe looked annoyed. "Will you two lovebirds leave the lovey-dovey crap for later? We need to figure out how to get out of here."

"We need to clear a path," Frank said. "We must figure out how to remove the snow in the driveway. Then we need to make a path for the truck."

"Let's get shoveling, and we might gun the engine and blast through it," Gloria replied.

"That will only work if we can get the truck up to speed," said Frank. "We have to do this fast." So he grabbed a shovel and started digging.

The air in the center of the parking lot swirled into a vortex, and a high-pitched, keening wail rose from its center. The wind picked up, whipping snow in every direction.

A narrow beam of light shot into the sky, turning dark and gritty. Then, the light beam raced upwards, widening until it surrounded a bright blue dot.

Barbara screamed, "We need to get back inside! Something is coming!"

"What is it?" Gabe said. "Tell me!"

That was when they all saw something running toward them, dragging a stream of white in its wake.

"It's coming!" Leah screamed. "Run!"

"Something huge!" Sam shouted.

A beast arose from the snow, hulking and massive. Snow flew up into a swirling cloud as it slammed against the pickup truck, which careened off the driveway into a gigantic tree with a tremendous, loud impact. The vehicle wobbled and fell to the ground like a giant redwood felled in the woods.

They were screaming and scrambling to get out of the way when it surged toward them, a massive shape dark against the snow. They ran, slipping on the icy ground, backtracking as the monstrous, wailing thing charged after them, a monster in the snow. Gabe and Frank tried to throw themselves in front of it, but it smashed them aside, forcing them to the ground.

Gloria and Sam bolted toward the diner, snow flying over their heads. The monster jumped behind them.

They ran into the restaurant, slamming the glass door behind them. They rushed to the window and peered out through the ice-covered glass.

Leah's boots sank deep into the soft spot that cracked beneath her. White, powdery snow rose to her waist and brushed against her face like strands of hair. Then, just as she was about to take another step into the deeper snow, the silence of the night broke.

The snow around her feet erupted. Then, with a sound like the air sucked from the ear, a dark shape barreled toward her, trampling the snow, crushing it into ice chips. It knocked Leah back, and she tumbled through the snow.

She fought to hold on to whatever she could grab, but as she spun in the air and felt herself drop, there was only cold and darkness.

Her body went limp, and whatever was touching her started picking her up, dragging her through the snow and deeper away from the diner. She didn't scream or try to fight. She knew it was over.

Something ripped into her. It tore her from her neck to her crotch, with blood squirting out in every direction. Blood pooled under her body, and she fell silent.

Nine

The Showdown

T HE DINER DOOR FLEW open, and out of the grey moonlight plunged Barbara, Frank, and Gabe. It closed behind them with a sharp bang.

Frank was hysterical. He kept saying, "No, no, no, no, no, no."

Gabe grabbed Frank by the shoulders, who turned and looked at Gabe, his eyes brimming with tears. He pointed toward a window and gasped, "It took my baby. She was right there." He shook his head and gripped Gabe's arms. "How many more are there?"

"Everyone! We need to stand our ground, or we will all die!" Gabe shouted. "We need to fight this thing and not run!"

"We saw that they can make us one of them," Gloria asked. "How do we even fight it? We are out of ammo. What if this is an alien attack?"

Barbara grabbed Gabe's arm. "I know one way we can kill that thing, but it would mean one of us would need to get close to it."

Gloria stopped pacing at gaped at Barbara. "I am game for anything at this point. So what is your idea?"

Barbara sniffled and wiped away tears. "Geno kept a hand grenade from when he was in the war in the kitchen. I guess he kept it as a memento or maybe some warped sense of security. I always hated that thing being in here, but now I guess sweet Geno is still looking out for me."

Gloria looked stunned. "Are you sure the grenade even works? How do you even use one?"

"It works. At least he said so," Barbara said, wiping her nose. "You just pull the pin, throw it, and run."

"So I would need to get close," Gloria said.

Sam looked terrified. "No, Gloria, I will!"

Suddenly, an enormous chunk of metal sailed through the diner's window, leaving a trail of broken glass behind it. It sliced through the empty seats and slammed into the metal counter. Screams joined a shrill whistle as the building took on a guttering moan. They dove to the floor and covered their heads as shards of glass rained around them.

"Where is the grenade?" Gloria shouted.

"In the kitchen above the counter," Barbara answered.

A blast of frigid wind and ice burst through the front door and swept over them.

Sam pushed himself up into a crawl and took shelter under the kitchen table, frozen where he lay. In front of him lay a pile of splintered wood covered in ice and snow. The floor buckled and cracked around the mound.

He stepped back and ran to the kitchen wall, where a laminated shelf was covered with pictures of Geno in his Army uniform. A single grenade, the size of a cantaloupe, was wedged between two photos. He grabbed it and slid under the barricade back into the dining room.

A colossal thing with a human-like shape but made of writhing, ropy arms and legs held Frank in the air by his throat.

Each of its long fingers ended in a writhing tentacle, and the pale, translucent skin between its suckers was slick with blood.

He watched the creature spin around towards him, dropping Frank. It shrieked at Sam and charged in his direction.

"No, Sam!" Gloria screamed.

Sam's heart hammered in his chest as he ran through the restaurant. Tables and chairs shattered against the walls as the beast pounded after him.

He skidded through the kitchen doorway, raising a cloud of powdered sugar with the kick of his boots, and hurried over to the other side of the swinging doors. The creature dove through the opening as he lunged towards the light. His hand closed around cold metal, and he tumbled through the doorway as the beast's hot breath washed over him.

The monster's snaking tendrils drew tight around Sam's mouth, muffling his cries. Sam tried to break free, but the beast tightened its grip. He didn't even have time to scream as it lumbered him away, further away from the diner into the shambling waves of snow.

His sweaty palm held the grenade's smooth, round handle. He opened his fingers, and warm metal slipped through them. He gritted his teeth and squeezed the object until his palm hurt.

He slowly slid the pin out of the grenade with his thumb. His left hand shook as he held the rough surface, a hand-drawn ring around the center, and dark threads of kapok that appeared to be burrowing inside themselves.

The creature's odor wafted toward him–a mixture of wet earth, rotten meat, and decay.

J.C. MOORE

"EAT THIS BITCH!" Sam screamed as he threw the grenade at the creature's mouth.

The explosion sent snow into the air and across the sky. Then, a moment later, as the snow was still blossoming, there was a tremendous thump as if a great weight was settling onto the earth.

"Sam!" Gloria screamed, dropping to her knees and crying.

Billows of smoke rose into the night sky, thick and black as tar. Rings of light, flickering and mesmerizing, danced through the smoke. Above their heads, circular flashing lights suspended in the air, pulsing in unison.

"What the hell is that?" Gabe whispered.

Two more spinning cylinders with flashing lights appeared out of nowhere and quickly shot up into the sky, disappearing into the night and leaving red and blue glowing trails behind them.

As the trails faded, the glow of yellow light from the street lamps above and the store windows grew more intense until it was all they could see. After that, they were just dark silhouettes bathed in soft light, shaking and crying as they held one another.

Ten

Epilogue

Emily's face was tear-streaked, and her bottom lip quivered. She hugged her grandmother's legs and sobbed, "Grandma, did Sam die?"

"Yes, he did. We were all saved by him. He sent that monster back to hell, but he died doing it. But he was a hero, and heroes go to heaven."

Emily twisted her body to the side to get close to her grandmother.

"What happened to everyone?" she asked.

"Well, when Sam didn't come back--" her grandmother hesitated, stroking Emily's hair. "They put us all in a hospital for a few weeks." She was quiet for a moment, remembering. "To make sure no one got sick from an infection."

YULETIDE INVASION

Seeing this bit of horror thrilled Emily. "Like, so that you didn't turn into an alien?" she said, bouncing up and down.

"Yes, honey."

The front door swung open. Emily leaped up, ran to them, and wrapped her arms around her mother's waist.

"We're home, honey," her father said. He turned toward his daughter and ruffled her hair.

Emily's mother grabbed the child's hand and walked toward the kitchen with her. "Hi Gloria, thank you for watching her while we shopped."

Gloria smiled. "Of course, Emily and I had a nice evening, didn't we?"

"Yeah. Grandma told me the story about the Christmas monsters."

Emily's mother put her arm around her daughter as they walked across the tile floor in the kitchen and slung the grocery bags onto a round oak table. She leaned down and kissed Emily on top of her head.

"Mom, you didn't scare her too much, did you?" Marcus asked.

"No, I didn't scare her. Did I, honey?" Gloria asked.

"No," Emily said.

"No, of course not," Gloria replied with a smile.

"Maybe your grandmother can tuck you in, Emily? Santa wants you to be a good girl, and tomorrow is Christmas. So I want to make sure you're up to getting your presents. Your father and I will be up late tonight wrapping gifts," Emily's mother said.

Emily's face spread into a broad smile and bounced up and down. "Okay!" she said.

"Well, I am going to take a shower and then I'm going to bed too, Emily," Gloria said. "I'm getting old, and I need my beauty sleep."

"Are you?" Emily asked. She paused for a moment and then frowned. "You're not old."

"Yes, I am," Gloria replied. "Good night, everyone."

"Good night," Marcus said. "Emily, did you say thank you to Grandma for watching you?"

"Thank you, Grandma."

"You're welcome. Let me tuck you in," Gloria said, patting the child on the cheek.

Gloria grabbed Emily's hand, and they walked upstairs to her bedroom.

Emily rushed to the bed and bounced up and down on her toes.

Gloria chuckled. "Well, all right. Lay down here and get under the blankets."

YULETIDE INVASION

Emily scrambled into bed, stretching out across the sizeable queen-size mattress, and she looked up at her grandmother with excitement.

Gloria sat on the edge, leaned over, and kissed Emily.

"Good night Grandma," Emily said.

Gloria closed the door to the little girl's room and was halfway down the hall when Emily called out to her. "Grandma!"

Gloria stopped and turned toward the voice. "What is it, honey?" she asked, walking back to her.

"Did you ever catch the infection? Did any of the other people get it?" Emily asked.

"No. No one did. We were all fine," Gloria said.

"Good," Emily said, rolling over to face the wall.

Gloria closed the door to the room and walked down the hall to the bathroom. She took a deep breath in front of the mirror and let her hair down, taking care to place her robe on the hook.

She turned on the shower and held her face to the warm stream. The water soaked her hair and made it hard to see through the white clouds. She ran her hand down her back and watched the tendrils rise and float across the room. She groaned and smiled.

The water rippled and whipped her hair over her back, and the flexible growths tickled her skin as they slithered over one another, making a thousand tiny animal sounds. She smiled, closed her eyes, and sang a Christmas carol, the tips of the tentacles gently touching the corners of her lips.

Afterword

In an effort to add some holiday horror to the world, I wrote Yuletide Invasion. The goal was to create a book that emulated the feeling of 1950s and 1960s alien invasion movies blended with the spirit of Christmas. Of course, to me, this meant no laser guns, advanced technology, or master computer.

The specific films I wanted to emulate were The Thing from Another World (1951), Earth vs. The Flying Saucers (1956), The Blob (1958), and Invasion of the Body Snatchers (1956).

I also am a giant fan of John Hughes movies from the 1980s. So I wanted to capture that in this story as well. So if you ever notice a similarity between my story and a John Hughes movie, don't be surprised.

J.C. MOORE

It seems like every Christmas story follows the same overused themes of a snowman that comes to life, a dead relative coming back as a Christmas ghost, an evil Santa, or a variation on the Gift Of The Magi. So the challenge was to write an original Christmas story.

I started by writing a short story. Then I made it into a full-length novella. It was super fun and quick to write. But, most of all, I hope that you, the reader, had fun reading it. I enjoyed writing it.

Until the next story, stay safe and keep reading.

J.C

November 2022

Acknowledgments

Writing books has been more challenging, rewarding, and grueling than I ever imagined. But, of course, none of this would have been possible without my wife, Heather. She has been by my side throughout my difficulties and celebrated my successes. That is genuine friendship.

My parents were always there to support me, as were my father, who taught me how to write and market, and my mother, who listened to me when I needed it.

My kids have reminded me that life is too short and sometimes you need to stop and enjoy it, and my dog Archie reminds me that sometimes those things that seem like nothing can be the most rewarding–like running through a snowdrift.

And finally, to YOU, the reader - without you, this entire process would be useless.

J.C.

If you enjoyed the story

If you enjoyed this story, please leave a review on Amazon and Goodreads. I read them all, and they are appreciated. They help me grow as a writer.

About Author

Award-winning author J. C. Moore is a published songwriter, father, husband, IT guy, and professional musician. His debut novel, "Hidden By The Dark," received the Silver Award in the Literary Titan Book Awards. He resides in upstate NY.

Also By

Hidden By The Dark: A gripping psychological thriller with a jaw-dropping twist (Pine Creek Thriller Book 1)

Something terrifying has awakened in the mountains... **A sheriff and his deputy investigate several brutal murders in a coal mining community where fear and terror have struck. As the investigation continues, they piece together a shocking and terrifying puzzle that leads him to believe**

that the murders may be the work of a serial killer. Or is it someone from out of town? Or worse yet, is there something even more sinister? The murders seem to have no pattern or motive, leaving them struggling to find answers. With time running out, the sheriff must find the killer before he strikes again.

Dead In The Shadows: A gripping psychological thriller with a breathtaking twist (Pine Creek Thriller Book 2)

There is an evil lurking in the dark, *and it has a taste for blood*. What starts as a simple camping trip turns into more than Emma bargained for when she witnesses her friends being attacked by a madman slashing his way through their group. As she watches her friends die in a series of increasingly terrifying attacks, Emma must fight to survive as she realizes there's something much bigger going on than just one killer hunting them down *one by one.*

Earth Rebels!: A Post Apocalyptic Survival Story

Aliens have invaded Earth and the fate of all humankind is not about an endless war against the countless hostile aliens and mutant species, but something far worse!

Death arenas, killer drones and new planets are only the beginning...

While they search for a new home - a new Earth, the few humans that have survived are fending for themselves in a hostile world.

Outnumbered and outgunned by the drones and human hunters sent by the Grey Ones, they must use all of their cunning and wits to survive.

One renegade fighter with an unlikely crew, and an aging ship the Avalon are all that stands between humanity and its destruction.